DANGER AT THE CIRCUS!

Sandy Creek
NEW YORK

An Imprint of Sterling Publishing
387 Park Avenue South
New York, NY 10016

ISBN 978-1-4351-5334-9

Translated by Glynne Yeardley

Editor: Shirley Willis

Manufactured in Heyuan, Guangdong Province, China
Lot #:
2   4   6   8   10   9   7   5   3   1
06/13

Alain Surget

Fabrice Parme

DANGER AT THE CIRCUS!

CHAPTER 1

THE FROG....

ALEXANDRIA, EGYPT 48 BC

Antinios felt very proud; his father had left him in charge of the shop while he was out pressing olives in the yard. Antinios was standing behind three huge clay pots that served as a counter. Each pot was filled with green or black olives. Suddenly, his pet fox, which had been dozing beside him, pricked up his ears and shot across the room like an arrow.

"What is it, Fenk? A mouse?"

It wasn't a mouse that Fenk had spotted but a frog that had come in through a little hole in the wall. The frog took flight when it saw the fox bounding toward it and leaped to the right, then the left to escape. Fenk darted after it in hot pursuit.

"Stop, Fenk! Stop!" Antinios yelled, terrified that the fox would knock over one of the olive pots or trip up a customer.

But Fenk took no notice and the frog was still leaping all over the shop.

"I'd better get that frog outside before they wreck the shop," sighed Antinios.

Following Fenk's example, he began leaping after the frog to try and drive it toward the door. Finding itself hunted from all sides, the frog panicked, made an enormous leap, and landed in one of the big pots.

"In the name of Zeus!" Antinios cried. "I'd better get it out of there before a customer comes in!"

But the frog had jumped into the pot of green olives.

"That was crafty! How am I going to find him now?"

He reached both arms down into the pot right up to his elbows and poked around with his hands to make the frog come out.

"I'll get you!" he shouted.

A horrified gasp made him look up. A woman wearing a neat white tunic was standing in front of him.

"What on earth are you doing? That's disgusting!" she protested.

The boy blushed scarlet as he pulled his oily arms out of the pot.

"I...I was just mixing the olives so that the ones at the bottom would get some light. It makes them more...um..."

The frog chose that exact moment to leap from the olive pot and landed right on the woman. She shrieked in terror and lurched backward as she tried to knock the creature off, but it was caught up in the folds of her tunic. Antinios came to help her.

"Don't touch me with those filthy hands! That wretched frog has already made enough mess of my lovely new tunic!"

She pushed the boy off, but Fenk thought that she was attacking his master and sank his teeth into her ankle.

At the sound of her screams, Antinios' father came rushing into the shop.

"What's all this commotion?" he demanded.

Fenk let go of the woman's ankle and slunk off to hide behind the olive pots.

"That's the last time I set foot in this shop! I shall be sure to tell all my friends not to come here either," shouted the customer angrily as she flounced out.

Shamefaced, Antinios explained what had happened. His father exploded with rage.

"After all you've done to save Caesar and Cleopatra, I thought you would be capable of looking after an olive shop for a few minutes! As you obviously can't manage that, I forbid you to hang around the palace with Cleo and Imeni ever again! And don't even think you'll be going to Rome with them after this!"

CHAPTER 2

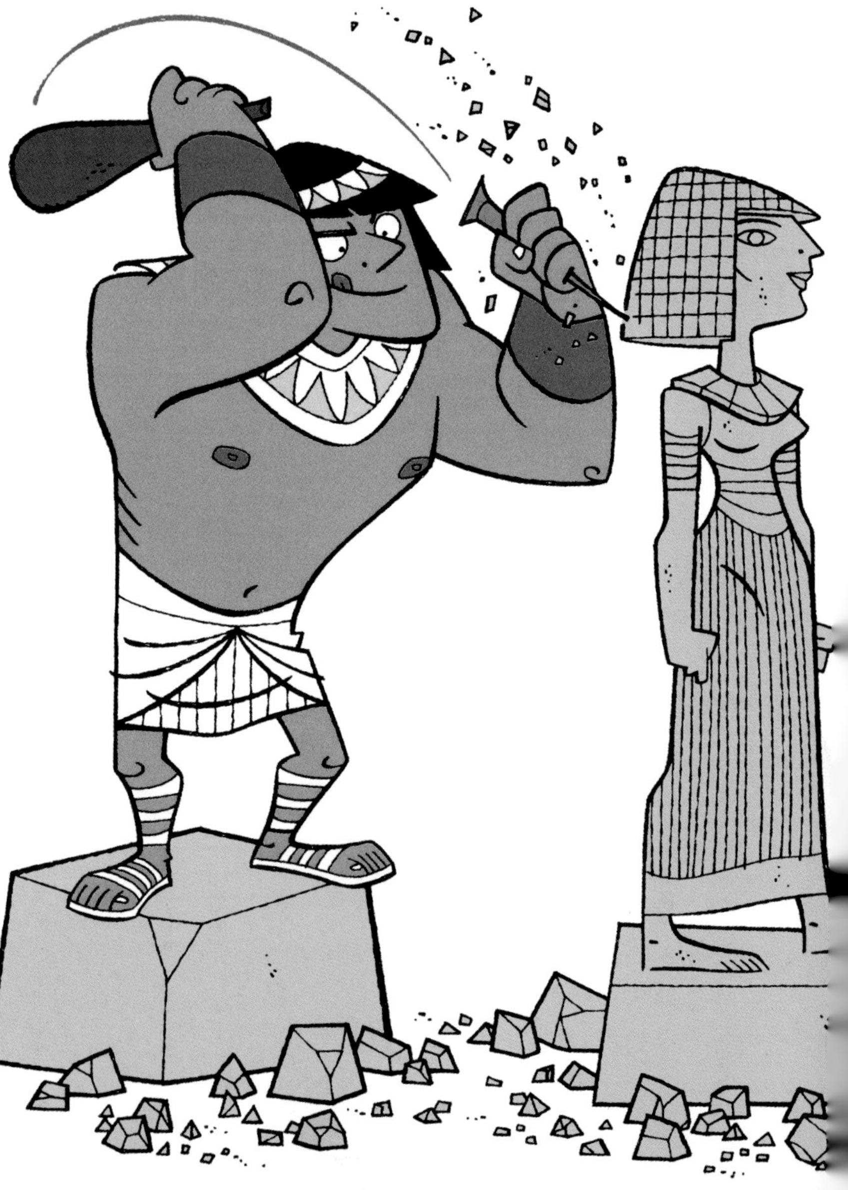

...AND THE BEAUTY SPOT

Tap! Tap! Tap! Imeni was watching attentively as his father sent tiny chips of marble flying all over the workshop. The statue had to be perfect; a rich papyrus merchant had ordered it for his wife's birthday.

"Can you see that the right cheek is still a little fuller than the left?" the mason asked his son. "Take your mallet and chisel and show me that you can carve properly now."

Imeni held his chisel up to the statue's face and looked for the correct angle to strike at the excess marble.

"You need to hit it with a single precise stroke!" his father reminded him.

"Just tap the chisel with your mallet."

A thin sliver of marble flew off the cheek.

"That's good. Keep it up!" his father said approvingly.

Little by little, Imeni shaped the cheek as if he were peeling it like an apple. His father stopped him when it was perfect.

"I've just got to polish it now," he said. "I'll go and get my polishing tools."

Alone in the workshop, Imeni paced around the statue. He was very proud of helping his father to make such a fine piece. The merchant would be very pleased and would tell all his friends, so they might get many more commissions. Suddenly he spotted a slight blemish. How could his father have missed that? How had that ugly little mark escaped his father's expert eye?

"It looks like a beauty spot under the nose!"

Imeni placed his chisel against the nose and tapped it. Nothing happened. He tried again. There was no shifting this blemish. Tap! This time he hit it harder. Just one precise stroke like his father said. The marble suddenly made a strange sound as

though it were cracking inside.

"For Osiris' sake. I hope I haven't damaged the nose!"

He grasped the nose between his fingers and tried it.

"No, it's fine."

But the head itself started moving. Imeni was stunned as he watched the neck split in two, then the head toppled forward as if it were saying hello. It was horrible! The head fell into his arms at the exact moment his father came back into the workshop.

Imeni's father cried out in dismay and flung his hands in the air.

He ran over and seized the statue's head from Imeni. He stared at it angrily, then he turned his furious gaze on his son.

"You idiot! What have you done? How can you be so clumsy?"

Imeni swallowed hard.

"I only meant to take off that wart-thing under its nose."

"Get out of my sight, you useless lump! And I thought you would soon be able to help me here. You've ruined several days' hard work. You'll be punished. From now on, you are not allowed to go and play with Antinios and Cleo. And don't even think about going to Rome with them either!"

Night had fallen over Alexandria. Everyone was asleep. Well, not quite everyone.

Cleo sighed. She had been waiting for her friends for ages. What could Antinios and Imeni be up to? Why were they so late? If they weren't able to see each other in the daytime, they usually met up at night down in the harbor, near the great lighthouse of Pharos.

"We're setting off for Rome the day after tomorrow," she grumbled, kicking at a stone. "What are they thinking?"

At last, two small figures appeared at the end of the harbor wall.

"That's them! Hmmph! They've certainly taken their time!" she muttered.

She rushed to meet her friends.

"We had to sneak out in secret," explained Antinios.

"And we're in for a good beating if our parents find out," Imeni added.

"But it gets worse," Antinios went on. "Neither of us is allowed to go to Rome now."

Cleo stared at them as if she'd been turned into the sphinx. Her eyes darted from one to the other.

"Why? What have you done?" she demanded. "That's a really harsh punishment!"

"Oh, it was all Fenk's fault!" said Antinios, hanging his head.

"And what about you?"

"Oooooh," Imeni raised his eyes to the heavens and gave such a long sigh that Cleo could only imagine the worst.

"So I'm going to be on my own then?" she blurted out crossly.

"It's all right for you," said Imeni. "You don't have any parents, so you can do what you want!"

"I've got my mother," she protested, "but I haven't heard from her since she sold me to the tavern keeper in Memphis. But I do miss her so much," her voice trailed away sadly.

They went quiet for a moment.

"All right then," said Cleo after a while, "I won't go to Rome either. I'll stay here with you."

Imeni fidgeted from one foot to the other.

"It's just that…"

"Our parents don't want us to see each other," Antinios finished for him. "Oh, they'll come around eventually, but right now…"

"But that's horrible!" protested Cleo. "What will we do if they keep us apart?"

"We can always meet here in secret at night," said Antinios, "but sneaking aboard a ship against our parents' wishes will be…"

"I won't give up yet," muttered Cleo. "I can't count on Cleopatra; she may be queen, but she won't go against your family's wishes. No, I'll have to do something else to change your fathers' minds. It always works!"

CHAPTER 3

THE SEA EAGLE

And work it did! The ship carrying Julius Caesar and Cleopatra, their attendants, and the three children sailed majestically out of the harbor. Three escort vessels followed in its wake. At the end of the jetty, Antinios' and Imeni's parents stood waving goodbye.

"There they go!" sighed Imeni's mother. "I do hope they're going to be all right!"

"They're in good hands," her husband reassured her. "Caesar and Cleopatra will keep them safe."

"All the same, but I do think you gave in very easily to that young woman who was sent by the queen."

"It was an order from Cleopatra!" he protested.

"Hmmm... she did have pretty kitty cat eyes

22

and a lovely velvety voice."

"Why, it sounds just like the woman who came to see us," said Antinios' mother. "My husband soon fell under her spell, too. He just couldn't say no!"

"Well, she promised me an assistant to help in the shop," the olive seller reminded her.

"She offered me an apprentice while Imeni was away," added the stonemason. "I wasn't going to refuse an offer like that!"

The three children were standing on the prow of the ship enjoying the feel of the fine spray being thrown up in their faces.

"So here we are, off on an adventure," said Cleo, smiling. "I knew my friend would be able to convince your parents. Everyone falls for Tamara's stories!"

"The thing that bothers me is that they'll never see those apprentices."

"We'll certainly hear about it when we get back home!"

"Forget about Alexandria!" Cleo advised. "Just make the most of the smell of freedom!"

The three of them puffed out their chests and filled their lungs.

"It smells mostly of fish," Imeni pointed out.

After two weeks of sailing over a flat, calm sea, the *Sea Eagle* reached some islands in the Bay of Naples in Italy.

Cleo yawned; she was bored. Since leaving Alexandria, she had found the forced idleness hard to bear, but what could she do? She couldn't very well climb the mast after all! Imeni was slumped beside her as lifeless as a bundle of rags, while Antinios was stroking Fenk, who was fast asleep on his lap. Caesar and Cleopatra were in their cabin and the oarsmen were stretched out on the deck, taking their break. Even the helmsman seemed to be dozing at the tiller. Cleo heaved a deep sigh and walked to the prow of the ship. The coast slid by on her right and she could see the rocky outlines of the islands straight ahead.

And then suddenly...!

"What's that moving in the water over there?"

She shaded her eyes with her hand; it looked as though large white butterflies had landed on the sea.

"They're ships! A whole fleet!"

The girl frowned. Where had these ships come from? They had suddenly sailed out from between the islands as though they had been hiding. They weren't heading for the coast but straight toward the *Sea Eagle*.

"It must be pirates!" she exclaimed.

She turned around, expecting to hear the captain raise the alarm, but nothing happened. A strange inertia reigned over the ship.

"Get to your oars!" she yelled. "We're under attack!"

Imeni and Antinios rushed to her side.

"There's about a dozen of them," said Antinios.

"They'll spear us like ducks on a spit," cried Imeni in panic.

"But why aren't our escort ships getting between us and the pirates?" asked the girl anxiously.

"Why aren't the men rushing back to their oars to escape?"

The three of them began yelling to wake the crew from their lethargy. The cabin curtain was pulled aside with some force and Caesar appeared wrapped in a red robe, the captain by his side.

"What's the reason for this racket?" cried the captain angrily.

One glance was enough for Caesar to understand why the children were so agitated.

"Calm down!" he told them. "Those are Roman ships. A few days before we left Alexandria, I contacted Mark Antony to tell him to send reinforcements from Rome. You are quite right; there are lots of pirates hiding in Sardinia, waiting to rob ships between there and Italy. But these ships are here to protect us."

The ships sailed closer. The water ahead of them seemed to boil, churned up by their enormous bronze boarding spikes. The flotilla fanned out to encircle the Egyptian vessels, then turned around to form an escort.

"We're as good as home now," said Antinios happily. "With an escort like that, no pirate would dare show his face."

"Rome must be very powerful," said Imeni. "They say there are shows every day in the Circus. But what is a circus exactly?"

"I have no idea," said Cleo. "But the best part is that we're so far from Egypt now. The plotter can't get to Cleopatra here. At last, we can really enjoy the trip now that we don't have to keep watch over her all the time!"

The next day, as they approached the port of Ostia, the ships had to converge together to enter the river Tiber that would take them to Rome. Cleopatra and Caesar were standing in front of their cabin watching the maneuvres. The ships were very close together and it took all the captains' expertise to stop the anchors from getting tangled. Orders rang out and the oars moved up and down. Suddenly, the *Sea Eagle* heeled over when one of the oarsman on the left side made a mistake. Caesar and Cleopatra were flung to one side just as an arrow planted itself in the side of the cabin, exactly where they had been standing!

Hearing the queen cry out, the soldiers threw themselves in front of her and Caesar and formed a barricade with their shields.

"Where did that shot come from?" bellowed Caesar.

Everyone turned to look at the group of ships to their right, but they were so close together that it

was impossible to say where the arrow had come from.

"Have all the ships tie up in Ostia!" ordered

Caesar. "I want to question all the captains and escort guards before we go on to Rome."

"It came from one of those ships that came to meet us," declared Cleopatra.

"Not necessarily," said Caesar. "It could have been someone who boarded in Alexandria and was waiting for the right moment to kill us."

"It's unbelievable!" groaned Antinios. "It's started again! We're not safe anywhere!"

"Our enemies are like weeds growing underfoot," marveled Imeni.

Cleo tried to look important as she declared,

"Once again, it will be up to us to keep our eyes and ears open. It's a good thing we are here!"

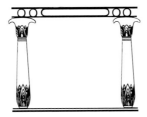

CHAPTER 4

THE CITY OF SEVEN HILLS

Julius Caesar banged on the table with his fist. He was furious! The sea captains and army officers were lined up in front of him. Nobody dared move.

"Not one of you saw a thing!" he demanded. "Neither the crew nor the guards! It's unbelievable! The assassin must be invisible! And we don't know whether I was the intended target or the queen of Egypt! Get back to your ships! Give orders to your sailors and soldiers to keep watch over each other! I shall hold you personally responsible if the assassin tries again."

He dismissed them. A voice came from behind.

"One of these men is a liar!"

A hand pulled aside the curtain that divided the

cabin in two and Cleopatra stepped out.

"I agree," muttered Caesar. "But who is it? Who is he working for? Is it a plot hatched in Egypt or in Rome?"

"We shall have to increase our security."

"Certainly, but we will not sneak into Rome like shadows. I want it to be a triumphant entry. I want to impress the Senate and the people. I want to hear the people of Rome calling out both our names."

"So you want to become a god then, is that it?" smiled the queen.

The ships sailed up the Tiber and moored near a bridge that faced the Great Gate of Rome.

"If the people like you, then Rome is yours," Caesar whispered to Cleopatra.

"Did you hear that?" murmured Cleo to her friends. "I think I'll try to conquer the Romans, too."

As soon as the soldiers disembarked, they hurried

toward the Great Gate. There, they lined up to form two rows in front of the gathered crowd, their shields held out before them.

"Gosh, it's like a double wall of breastplates leading right into the heart of the city!" exclaimed Imeni.

"Caesar is not taking any chances," said Antinios, "and I don't blame him. The marksman may very well be among the crowd, and he might try again—who knows?"

Caesar, who was standing on a chariot pulled by two white horses, set off slowly along the road into Rome. Behind him followed Cleopatra. She was seated on a throne made of exotic woods that was set between the feet of a huge solid gold sphinx. The giant wheeled structure was pulled along by forty men and was preceded by troupes of dancers and musicians that led it through the Great Gate into the city.

Huge crowds lined each side of the avenue. They were waving palm branches as Caesar and the queen of Egypt went by. The people cheered

Cleopatra, greeting her as if she were a goddess among them. She dazzled the crowd with her smiles and friendly gestures. Standing behind the sphinx, Cleo too was waving and smiling to attract the crowd's attention.

"You're wasting your time," Imeni told her. "The Romans only have eyes for Cleopatra and the golden sphinx."

"That's because they can't see me properly because you and Antinios are in the way! Go and stand at the side so you can watch the crowd!"

For a moment Cleo, intoxicated with all the cheering and music, cast her eyes across the city beyond. On Rome's seven hilltops, she could see splendid villas and white marble temples. Down in the valleys, it was a different story; the buildings were crowded together and the streets were so narrow and winding that she could hardly make them out. Only the avenues leading to the Forum were wide and straight. Suddenly, Antinios was back beside her.

"I've just seen someone weird," he told her.

"He's been threading his way steadily through the crowd, following us ever since we entered Rome. There he is; next to that woman waving her arms—yes, that one over there!"

"I can see him," said Cleo. "What a strange face—his nose looks like an eagle's beak. Keep Imeni with you. It will be easier for the two of you to keep an eye on him."

Suddenly Caesar quickened his pace and galloped straight toward a tribune, a raised gallery in the Forum, where three hundred senators were seated waiting for the queen.

"Ave Baltus!" he called down from his chariot to the oldest man.

Baltus acknowledged him with a nod.

"A fine show you've brought us," he muttered, as dancers appeared at the far end of the avenue. "Anyone would think we were at the Circus!"

"Make a good impression on the queen of Egypt," Caesar advised him.

"The people have never cheered so loudly before, even to welcome home victorious generals," said Baltus. "Don't expect us to fall at Cleopatra's feet! We Romans don't bow to anyone!"

"I'm not asking you to, but please drop that haughty expression. The Senate looks like a gathering of crows!"

When the golden sphinx reached the Forum, Antinios and Imeni spotted the mysterious man, walking alongside them again.

"Do you think the soldiers have spotted him, too?" asked Imeni.

"I'm not sure," answered Antinios. "We have a good view of the crowd from up here but the soldiers don't. Anyway, perhaps he just wants a better look at the queen."

Suddenly the music stopped as Cleopatra drew up in front of the three hundred senators. Old Baltus got to his feet and the other senators followed his lead. He greeted the young woman with these words:

"Welcome to Rome! Our city is very pleased to welcome the queen of Egypt as she passes through Rome."

"Passes through?" thought Cleopatra, raising an eyebrow. "Is old baldy already thinking of sending me packing back to Alexandria?" She inclined her head to thank him, then stood up and turned to the people.

"I intend to present Rome with a splendid gift!" she declared, interrupting Baltus, who was just about to continue his speech. "I want the people of Rome to have this solid gold sphinx! This alone is enough to pay for feasting and festivals for a whole year!"

The citizens of Rome roared with joy. Cleopatra's name was on every tongue, and the guards had

great difficulty restraining the crowds as they surged forward to try and carry the queen off in triumph. The senators sat down again. Baltus glanced angrily at Caesar.

"That woman has bewitched them," he growled. "She has charmed the people in an instant. She seems to have forgotten that in Rome, power lies with the Senate. If she has any evil intentions, she could prove extremely dangerous for our republic."

"You see evil everywhere, Baltus. Cleopatra has no desire to become queen of Rome."

"Be that as it may, we must keep this woman away from the people. It would be better to have her stay out of town on the other side of the river. You have a villa there, don't you? We didn't chase the Etruscan kings out of Rome only to let the queen of Egypt in."

Before Caesar had a chance to object, he added, "Don't let her stay too long!"

"Watch your words, senator!" snapped Caesar. "I won't tolerate lack of respect for Cleopatra!"

"You see! We are already arguing because of

her!" grumbled Baltus. "We must not let this woman divide us!"

Standing between the front paws of her golden sphinx, Cleopatra's gaze wandered over the crowd. Her eyes moved from one face to another without focusing on any one in particular. Not even the man with the hooked nose, who was watching her so intently.

CHAPTER 5

THE MAN WITH THE HOOKED NOSE

Cleopatra's fury resounded through the house. She had been dispatched to the other side of the Tiber, outside of the city; she had the distinct impression that they were trying to shun her.

"A fine welcome this is!" she cried as she paced back and forth. "First they greet me with arrows and now they isolate me here as if I, the ruler of Egypt, have a disease!"

"The Senate is afraid that the people admire you too much," explained Caesar. "They fear that you might use the people's goodwill against them."

"What have I possibly got to do with those bald headed senators? I didn't come to Rome to seize power. I'll leave that to you!"

They were in the atrium, an inner courtyard with a small pool in the center. Caesar was leaning against a column, waiting for the queen to calm down. The three children were with them. They were playing a game of five bones while listening to every word of this discussion. Cleopatra was standing in front of Caesar, wagging her finger in his face.

"I wouldn't be at all surprised if it were Baltus who ordered someone to shoot me."

"Don't be ridiculous!"

"What do you mean? Do you think I imagined that arrow? Or was it the gods who fired it?"

"Mark Antony is leading the investigation. He'll find the culprit and when he does, I'll have him thrown to the lions."

Caesar put his arm around Cleopatra's shoulders.

"Come with me and relax in the garden," he coaxed her. "Tomorrow I shall organize a great show at the Circus. You will be my guest of honor and the Romans will love you."

"Perhaps Cleopatra is right," mused Antinios.

"The Senate didn't give us a very warm welcome. Perhaps they really don't want us in Rome."

"The queen may find herself back in Alexandria before she expected," surmised Cleo.

"Well, as long as we have time to see the games at the Circus," sighed Imeni. "What exactly is a circus anyway?"

But no one answered.

Someone was knocking at the door. A servant hurried to open it and then crossed the atrium followed by a man. Cleo seized Antinios by the arm.

"It's him …the hooked-nose man," she hissed.

The children were astonished.

"It's definitely him," whispered Antinios. "What's he doing here?"

"He's planning to stab Cleopatra," gasped Cleo. "I'm sure he has a dagger hidden in his tunic!"

"Let's go into the garden and walk over to him as though nothing is wrong." said Cleo. "If we see anything suspicious, we can jump on him. That will give Caesar time to react."

"Hold on a minute," cautioned Antinios. "He's not going to attack the queen or Caesar in front of the servants."

"How do you know? Killers can be very daring people."

"Perhaps he's just here to assess where everything is so he can come back tonight with his bow and arrows," said Cleo. "Let's follow him!"

They went into the garden. It was a beautiful place planted with shrubs and flowers. Set between two fountains was a pool filled with large lily pads. The servant pointed to a bench by the edge of the pool.

"Please take a seat," he said to the stranger. "I'll tell Cleopatra that you are here."

The servant went off to find the queen, who was lying in the shade of a vine-covered trellis. The children, meanwhile, pretended to be playing with Fenk, pushing him little by little toward the hooked-nose man. He turned toward them and glared, then shifted his gaze toward the trellis, awaiting the servant's return.

However it wasn't the servant who reappeared but Cleopatra herself. She had decided to go back to her apartment. A smile lit up the man's face. He stood up.

"The queen is alone," whispered Cleo, whose heart was thumping fast. "Caesar must have stayed behind to speak to the servant."

The man bowed to Cleopatra.

"You asked to see me," she said.

He responded by putting his hand inside his tunic.

"Aaaargh!" screamed the three children as they hurled themselves at him.

The collision knocked the man clean off his feet and into the pool with the three children on top of him. Once she had recovered from her surprise, Cleopatra burst out laughing while Fenk was yapping as loudly as he could, too afraid to follow his friends into the water.

"What is going on now?" shouted Caesar, who had heard all the commotion.

He rushed in to find a man in the pool, loudly protesting that he could not swim. With the help of two gardeners, Caesar pulled the man out.

"He's an assassin," Cleo told him. "He was about to bring out his dagger!"

"This man is Cicero!" declared Caesar. "He's the most famous lawyer in all Rome!"

"That may be, but he was trying to kill Cleopatra!" cried Imeni. "He's got a dagger hidden in his tunic."

"I have not!" protested Cicero once he got his breath back. "It's a scroll!"

He proceeded to take out a dripping, rolled-up scroll and showed it to the queen.

"It concerns a text about some ancient laws I wanted to discuss with you. But after this…"

He flung the scroll angrily into the water.

"All Rome shall learn how you have treated me!" he assured them.

The children hung their heads in shame as they tried to explain themselves to the lawyer.

"We thought you were acting suspiciously this morning as you followed us through the crowd," explained Antinios. "So when you put your hand inside your tunic…"

"These children were simply trying to protect me," said Cleopatra. "You must forgive them. But why were you following us?"

Cicero merely shrugged his shoulders in reply and asked to be given dry clothes to go back to his home on the Capitoline Hill.

"Come back whenever you wish," said Cleopatra. "I'd be very happy to speak with you."

"We've made another enemy," said Caesar as Cicero followed a servant into the villa. "He's an important man. We really didn't need that!"

He gave the children an angry glare and went back inside without another word.

"How could we have known?" wailed Cleo.

"I think Cicero was more upset by my laughter than by being knocked over," confessed Cleopatra.

"These Romans are so sensitive."

"He didn't answer your question," said Imeni. "We still don't know why he was following us."

The queen dismissed his words with a wave of her hand.

"Oh, he was probably just curious to see what I look like. I shall soon win him over."

Her footsteps were light as she almost danced back into the villa.

"Cicero might still be plotting behind our backs," said Antinios warily.

"Let's follow him when he leaves, once he's changed his tunic," suggested Cleo. "We can see whether he contacts anyone. If he does, we can listen to what they say."

"But then we'd be in Rome all by ourselves," said Imeni fearfully.

Neither of his companions could think of anything reassuring to say. They knew very well what risks they were taking but they were ready to do anything to protect Cleopatra.

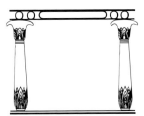

CHAPTER 6

LOST IN SUBURIA

It was late afternoon as Cleo, Imeni, Antinios, and Fenk walked back up the avenue leading to the Forum. Cicero, who was a little way ahead of them, was fending off the beggars and peddlers who tried to approach them. The Forum was lined with shops and was very crowded. Cries and shouts filled the air.

"Let's get closer to Cicero. We don't want to lose him among all these people."

As the children elbowed their way past idling shoppers, they narrowly avoided knocking over some joints of beef roasting on the butchers' grills. "Those kids are still following me," thought Cicero. "They are certainly persistent." His lips curved into a cunning smile. "I shall march right through town and wear them out. They'll certainly remember this walk for a long time; perhaps it will put them off meddling in other people's affairs." He led them up the Via Sacra past temples, covered markets, and other official buildings, then he turned off into the area called Suburia, where the poorest of Rome's people lived.

"Where is he going?" asked Imeni nervously as the streets became more and more narrow.

The cramped alleys were lined with two-story, windowless buildings and seemed more and more like dark twisting tunnels. The evening light only reached the rooftops, and the little streets below were draped in blue shadows.

"I don't like this place," whispered Imeni. "These streets are so narrow that I feel as if I'm suffocating."

"If he's coming here instead of going home, he must be up to something," guessed Antinios.

"Let's hold hands," said Cleo, seeing several suspicious characters lurking in doorways.

These shadowy figures watched the children as

they passed by. Some just muttered, but others took pleasure in scaring the children by reaching out and touching them.

"I want to go home," whimpered Imeni in a choked voice.

Glancing back, the children saw that the street behind was now thronged with people. As soon as night fell, bands of men and women roamed the streets looking for trouble. There was no turning back! They hurried on through a maze of alleyways until Cicero disappeared into a tavern called The Red Lantern.

"What do we do now?" wondered Antinios. "We aren't allowed in a place like this."

"We need to find out who Cicero is meeting," Cleo reminded them. "We'll have a quick look in to see who he is talking to and come straight out. Then if we wait until his accomplice leaves the tavern, we can follow him to find out where he lives and who he is."

It was Antinios who pushed open the tavern door. He was met by the greasy smell of fried food and the sound of lots of voices.

Men were slouched at tables with their noses in their drinking cups; some stared at the children but quickly lost interest. Four girls were playing flutes and tambourines but no one was really listening to the music.

"I can't see Cicero," said Imeni.

"Perhaps he's in another room…"

A huge hand grabbed Cleo by the shoulder.

"Well, are you going to dance for us, girlie?"

"Let me go!" she cried as she struggled to free herself.

Antinios and Imeni managed to push the man away. Fenk leapt at his ankle and he bellowed with rage.

"That's enough!" yelled a woman's voice.

In front of a stove stood an enormous woman with hands on her hips.

"Leave the girl alone!" she thundered. "And you three clear off! There's nothing for kids here! And take that animal with you – this isn't a circus I'm running!"

The man flopped back onto his seat and swallowed his wine in one gulp. A servant girl placed a plate of fried fish down in front of him.

"A man came in just before us," hissed Cleo to the servant girl. "Do you know where he is sitting?"

"He just walked straight through," she replied, pushing back a stray lock of hair. "He went out the back way."

She pointed to a corridor that led to a low doorway. Cleo ran down the passage with the two boys hard on her heels, but Cicero was long gone.

"He's tricked us!" she groaned.

"He must have spotted us," said Antinios.

"What now then?" demanded Imeni.

The alleyway looked deserted except for a dog nosing through the trash. The flaming torches that hung above the doors cast eerie dancing shadows on the walls.

"If we go around the block we'll find ourselves back at the front door of the tavern," suggested Antinios. "Then we only have to go back down the way we came. We're bound to recognize some of the buildings."

They went down the alleyway, took two left turns, cut through a narrow passage that they thought was a short cut, and found themselves in the inner courtyard of a bakery. They turned back and came into a little square with a horse trough. A gang of ruffians spotted them and started throwing stones. The children ran off to the sound of raucous laughter, only to find themselves lost in a tangle of alleyways.

"All these alleys look the same," gasped Antinios. "I can't tell where I am!"

"Rome is spinning a web around us," groaned Imeni. "We'll never find our way out of this labyrinth."

"We'd better not ask anyone the way," said Cleo. "They can't all be thieves, but let's not take the risk."

Shadowy shapes in the darkness forced them to change direction several times, driving them deeper into Suburia. Frightened and thirsty, they finally found a shed on the side of a basket weaver's shop.

"Let's hide here," said Antinios. "We'll set off again in daylight."

They slipped in among stacks of old broken baskets and stretched out side by side, exhausted. Just then, a terrifying shadow fell across them.

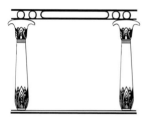

CHAPTER 7

NIGHT OF
THE SHE-WOLF

67

The three children let out such a scream of terror that the figure leapt backward.

"Sshh, don't make such a racket!" hissed an old woman. "We mustn't attract attention. I don't want to be driven out. I feel safe here at night under these baskets. The she-wolf will never come looking for me here."

"The she-wolf? What she-wolf?" asked Imeni in amazement.

"The Capitoline she-wolf, the one who suckled Romulus and Remus," she croaked.

"But that was centuries ago!" said Antinios. "She's been dead for years."

"No, no, she prowls around the city at night, sniffing under doors..."

"That must be dogs!"

"She creeps into yards, knocking things over…"

"That's just cats!"

"Sometimes she makes a dreadful sound fit to wake the dead."

"That's just a donkey braying!"

"You fools!" cried the woman, shaking Antinios by his shoulder. "It's the she-wolf, I tell you, the she-wolf! By day she takes the form of a statue in front of the temple of Jupiter to watch what people are up to. But at night she steps down from her marble plinth and wanders all over Rome. Woe to anyone who crosses her path! She devours them with one bite. Just like that!" she added with a click of her tongue. "Listen! Can't you hear the wolf's footsteps?"

"That's rain pattering on the tiles. It's just begun to rain."

"It's the she-wolf; it's the she-wolf! She's coming. Get out of here! There's no room for you! Clear off or I'll poke you with my stick!"

"Tell us how to get back to the Forum," said

Cleo, "then we'll leave you in peace."

The old woman quickly told them which way to go. She rubbed her hands together as she watched them walk away.

"Good," she mumbled. "If the wolf catches those three, she won't come prowling around here for a while."

The streets gradually widened until the children reached a road lined with flaming torches that led to the Forum.

"That old woman may be a bit mad but she certainly knows the city," said Imeni, pleased to be back among temples and shops again.

His eyes fell on the brooding mass of the Capitol. Sacred fires burned in front of the temple of Jupiter, outlining its shape in the darkness and… the statue of the she-wolf! Staring at it, Imeni couldn't help but imagine the creature baring its teeth ferociously.

"To think that the mad old woman believes it comes to life…."

He tried to laugh, but a feeling of anxiety overwhelmed him. At that very moment, a long howl seemed to echo down from the hills—an eerie sound that ended with a bark. A cold shudder ran down his spine.

"It's the she-wolf!" he cried. "She's woken up!"

"It's just the wind!" Antinios told him. "It's whistling through the columns."

"And that's a dog...."

The howling slowly built up all around them from the surrounding hills. The sound rose up to the heavens again and again like an evil omen.

"It really is wolves," stammered Cleo, her voice trembling. "We can't get back to Caesar's house tonight or they may attack us. We'll have to spend the night in Rome."

"In Rome?" cried Imeni in alarm. "But where?"

"Let's go to the Flumentana gate and ask to have shelter in the guardhouse," suggested Cleo.

That sounded like a good idea. Alas, when they arrived at the city wall, no matter how hard they yelled, the soldiers turned a deaf ear; they had no desire to put themselves out for a bunch of kids. It was raining hard now, almost a downpour. The children ran through the deserted streets looking for somewhere to find shelter.

"This way!" cried Antinios. "There are some arches!"

They hurried over, but the arches were filled with shops.

"What a strange building!" remarked Imeni. "It's not a temple or a market-hall. It looks like an enormous barrack, but it's not that either."

"That's the Circus!" cried Antinios. "My father told me about it."

"Has your father been to Rome then?"

"No, but being a merchant he has met lots of Romans. The Circus is where they have chariot races, wrestling, and wild animal fights. Sometimes, if the spectators don't like what they see, they climb into the arena and then it's chaos."

"My hair is wet and my dress is soaked—I must look a real mess," complained Cleo.

"Well, your hair is a bit frizzy with the rain," Imeni told her, "but you look more like a …."

A sharp dig in the ribs from Antinios silenced him. Cleo glared at Imeni and without another word, he followed his friends. Just then, they came across a small door in the wall. Cleo leaned against it and to her surprise, it opened and revealed a tunnel leading right into the Circus.

"Let's see exactly where it goes," said Antinios.

"We're not going in there!" protested Imeni. "It's as dark as Seth's lair!"

"Wait for us here in the rain then," snapped Cleo. "You can't get much wetter. You already look like a drowned rat!"

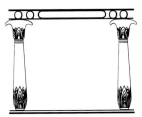

CHAPTER 8

IN THE HEART OF THE GREAT CIRCUS

A faint light was flickering at the end of the tunnel, guiding the children toward it. Suddenly, Fenk began to snarl.

"He can smell something," whispered Antinios, bending down to pick up the fox.

"Should we go back?" ventured Imeni.

A shove from behind urged him forward.

"Do you think there's someone there, Antinios?" whispered Cleo.

They could just hear a faint murmur of voices. As they crept quietly forward, they could hear Caesar's name being mentioned.

"There's something strange going on here," whispered Cleo.

The three children tiptoed along in single

file until they reached a room filled with racing chariots. Two men were working on an upturned chariot by torchlight; the children could hear the rasping sound of a file. A third man, an officer, was watching them at work.

"Don't make it too deep," he advised. "We don't want it to break as soon as the wheel turns. We'll have to sabotage the rest of your team's chariots," he said, turning to a fourth man. "It must be you and you alone who triumphs against Caesar tomorrow. When he offers you the laurel wreath, you will pierce his heart with your arrow. The bow and arrows are already hidden behind a false compartment in your chariot."

"What do I do if he decides to give the laurel wreath to Cleopatra instead?"

"I'll be alongside him. I'll remind him that the gods always insist that the winner's laurels must be given to a man. Once Caesar is dead, Cleopatra won't waste any time getting back to Alexandria. Once I get rid of Mark Antony, Rome will be mine!"

"You're reckoning without the Senate, General Cassius."

"I have friends in the Senate who will help me bring the rest of them into line."

The children overheard everything as they hid in the darkness. Cleo tapped each of her friends on the arm to signal that it was time to leave. Fenk chose that very moment to give another low growl in the back of his throat.

"Did you hear that?" asked one of the men.

"It came from the tunnel!"

Cassius unsheathed his sword.

"They're coming," cried Imeni. "If they catch us, they'll kill us!"

"They'll hear us if we run. The tunnel is too long and dark for us to get out before they catch up with us."

The children set off carefully, their hands groping along the walls until suddenly, there was nothing there! Another passage opened up to the side of the tunnel and they dove into it just as the torchlight leapt behind them. After a few yards, they came to a door. Fortunately, it was not locked!

"There's no one in the tunnel," said a man's voice.

"Search everywhere!" insisted the general. "If anyone is in here, he must not get away."

Cleo and the boys found themselves in a room that smelled strongly of animals. The torchlight behind them lit up the passage walls and they could hear their pursuers' footsteps getting closer.

The children quickly squeezed in behind a large crate; Antinios grasped Fenk's muzzle to stop him from barking, but he shouldn't have bothered. A terrible roar shook the room as the four men came rushing in.

An enormous bear had just woken up inside the crate. Seeing the intruders, he clawed viciously at the bars to drive them away.

"It must have been that beast's snoring we heard," said Cassius, putting his sword back in its sheath. "Let's get out of here! We haven't finished sabotaging the steering or the wheels yet."

The light drifted away as the door closed, but this time the bar was pulled across it so that the door couldn't be opened from the inside.

"We're trapped!" gasped Cleo. "They won't come to feed the bear till tomorrow. We won't be able to save Caesar!"

CHAPTER 9

URANUS

The next day, Caesar and Cleopatra were about to pass through the Flumentana Gate when a troop of horsemen stopped in front of them.

"What news?" asked the queen, anxiously.

"We've found no trace of the children," said their leader sadly.

"I'm sure they followed Cicero yesterday. Have you questioned him?"

The man nodded.

"He says that he led the children into Suburia to teach them a lesson. We questioned the keeper of the tavern that Cicero led them to, but she didn't see them again after they left."

"They must have lost their way in that part of town," said Caesar. "Keep looking! They're very independent, those three." Turning to Cleopatra, he added, "They'll turn up soon; don't worry. You never know, they're probably already waiting for us at the Circus!"

Cleo, Antinios, and Imeni were sitting behind bales of straw, desperate for the door to open. They could see daylight beyond the grill that separated the Circus arena from the bear's crate.

"We must be underneath the stands," guessed Antinios. "This is the way the wild beasts run into the arena."

Beyond the caged bear, the children could see spectators beginning to arrive. By the time Caesar and Cleopatra took their seats in the tribune facing the main entrance, all the stands were full. Cleo began yelling to attract attention but could not make herself heard over the noise of the spectators. Only the bear heard her and began shaking the bars of his crate.

"Don't upset him," pleaded Imeni. "If he breaks down those bars, he'll kill us."

Suddenly they heard a noise like thunder!

Twelve chariots had burst out of the starting gates.

"That's it then!" sighed Cleo. "We can't help Caesar now."

Whips cracked and the chariots, each pulled by four horses, began to whirl around the central arena. Cheered on by the spectators, the race got faster and faster, the horse's hooves hammering the ground. The Green team was in the lead, but one of their charioteers took a turn too tightly. The chariot behind crashed into one of its wheels. Both chariots swayed and almost overturned. The second charioteer pulled on his right hand rein to alter his horse's course. He'd managed to avoid a collision, but his rivals had managed to overtake him.

Each time a chariot threatened to crash or a wheel struck the central stone plinth, Cleopatra gripped Caesar's hand.

A loud "Oooooh!" erupted in the Circus.

A steering shaft had given way. The horses kept on running as the chariot and its driver slammed into the wall. At every lap, either a wheel would fall off, an axle would snap, or the bottom would fall out of a chariot.

Cassius, who was sitting beside Caesar, didn't take his eyes off his own man. "He's still behind but he'll complete all seven laps. The other chariots will fall apart before the end of the race."

From inside the bear's locked enclosure, the children counted the laps. They had no idea which charioteer was the assassin, though they tried to work it out.

"There are only five chariots left in the race now and this is the sixth lap," reckoned Antinios.

Imeni moved away from the bear's crate. He felt devastated by the thought that Caesar was about to die and no longer wanted to watch the race through the grill. He sat on a beam jutting out from the wall and yelled as it gave way under him.

There was a clanking of chains and the grill at the front of the crate lifted, giving access to the arena. The bear was taken by surprise but then stepped out into the arena. It shook itself and then began to shamble over to the horses galloping toward him.

The crowd was astonished by this surprising turn of events, but as the bear raked at the first chariot with his claws, they began chanting, "Uranus! Uranus!"

"What on earth is going on?" demanded Caesar. "Who opened that grill? Who dares disrupt the race like this?" He turned to Cassius. "Find some men with lances to get that animal back in its cage!"

"It would be easier just to kill it."

"No! I want to see Uranus fight an elephant at the next games."

Cassius froze. The three children had followed the bear out into the arena just at the very moment that Uranus charged his accomplice's chariot.

Cassius's eyes darted from the children to the charioteer, who was struggling to drive the bear off with his whip.

"Well," snapped Caesar. "What are you waiting for?"

Suddenly, Cleopatra was on her feet.

"Look. Over there!" she exclaimed. "Cleo, Imeni, and Antinios! They must have spent the night in the Circus....with a bear!"

"That's it!" thought Cassius. "With the race suspended, my man won't get near the tribune to kill Caesar. It must have been those kids who were in the chariot workshop. They've obviously heard everything or they wouldn't have run away. I can't keep them quiet with all of Rome watching. I'd better leave before they start talking."

Out in the arena, Uranus floored Cassius's accomplice with one swipe of his huge paw. Soldiers ran into the arena to protect the children. And Cassius, ignoring Caesar's orders, ran through the stands and came back into the arena at ground level near the starting gates. He was hoping to leave the Circus through the main entrance but, hearing the sound of hooves behind him, he turned to see four horses bearing down on him dragging what remained of his accomplice's empty chariot! He tried to escape but was trampled under their hooves.

"....and when the bear ran into the arena, we followed him out."

As Cleo finished her account of their escapade, Caesar shook his head in disbelief and Cleopatra smiled.

"We found the bow and arrows in a secret

compartment in his chariot," Caesar told them. "Cassius was part of the escort sent by Mark Antony. He gave the order to shoot at us. Some of his accomplices are still at large, but they won't dare try anything else now that their leader is gone."

"Rome is no better than Alexandria!" said Cleopatra. "There are traitors everywhere. It's fortunate that we have the best bodyguards in the whole world."

"That's right," said Caesar. "You three are worth all of our soldiers put together. You deserve a reward!"

He opened a small box and beckoned to the children. He gave each of them a small bee made of gold.

"These are the Daughters of Light. May they, in turn, protect you!"

There was a yapping sound.

They turned to see Fenk gazing at them imploringly.

"You want something, too," said the queen sympathetically.

She bent down, picked up the fox, and placed him in her lap.

"That's the kind of reward half the world is longing for," smiled Caesar. Fenk purred happily as Cleopatra fondly caressed him.

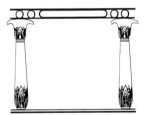

ABOUT THE AUTHOR

Alain Surget is a professor of history as well as a prolific novelist. He started writing plays and poetry at the early age of 14, then went on to write more than 130 novels and other books. His first sight of the Pyramids and images of the Pharaohs sparked a lifelong interest in Ancient Egypt. Many of his novels are set there.

Alain is married with three children and lives in Gap in France. Despite writing about the adventures and travels of his characters—who are often feisty heroines—Alain admits to being an armchair traveler himself!

ABOUT THE ILLUSTRATOR

Fabrice Parme was born near Nancy in France. After finishing Art School in Angoulême, he moved to Paris, where he worked as an illustrator for various magazines, including comic and "graphic novel" style, and for television. His illustrations for the Children of the Nile series are the first he has done for children's books.